ANTZ

JUNIOR NOVELIZATION

ANTZ

JUNIOR NOVELIZATION

by **Ellen Weiss**
based on the animation screenplay
by **Todd Alcott** and **Chris Weitz** & **Paul Weitz**

PUFFIN BOOKS
Published by the Penguin Group
Penguin Putnam Books for Young Readers, 345 Hudson Street,
New York, New York 10014, U.S.A.
Penguin Books Ltd, 27 Wrights Lane, London W8 5TZ, England
Penguin Books Australia Ltd, Ringwood, Victoria, Australia
Penguin Books Canada Ltd, 10 Alcorn Avenue, Toronto, Ontario, Canada M4V 3B2
Penguin Books (N.Z.) Ltd, 182-190 Wairau Road, Auckland 10, New Zealand

Penguin Books Ltd, Registered Offices: Harmondsworth, Middlesex, England

Published by Puffin Books,
a member of Penguin Putnam Books for Young Readers, 1998

1 3 5 7 9 10 8 6 4 2

Printed in the United States of America

CHAPTER

The psychologist's office was calm and serene, and the patient lay comfortably on the couch. He had been here many times.

Outside, the jangling sounds of the big city were dimly audible.

"All my life," the patient was saying, "I've lived and worked in the big city. Which is kind of a problem, since I always feel uncomfortable around crowds. I have this fear of enclosed spaces. Everything makes me feel trapped all the time. I keep telling myself there's got to be something better out there, but maybe I think too much."

He rearranged his feelers and continued. "I think

everything must go back to the fact that I had a very anxious childhood. You know, my mother never had time for me. When you're the middle child in a family of five million, you don't get a lot of attention."

The psychologist clasped his forelegs, leaning forward to listen intently. "Mmm-hmmm," he said.

"And I've always had these abandonment issues which plague me," the patient continued. "My father was basically a drone. The guy flew away when I was just a larva. And my job—don't get me started."

The patient was getting himself all worked up now, his antennae bobbing in agitation. "I was not cut out to be a worker. I'll tell you right now. I feel physically inadequate. My whole life, I've never been able to lift more than ten times my own body weight. And, when you get down to it, handling dirt is not my idea of a rewarding career. It's this whole gung-ho 'superorganism' thing that I can't get. I try but I don't get it. I mean, I'm supposed to do everything for the colony—but what about *my* needs? What about me? I mean, I've got to believe there's someplace out there that's better than this. The whole system just makes me feel so—*insignificant.*" He paused for breath, exhausted by this outpouring of emotion.

The psychologist, however, was very excited. "Excellent!" he cried. "You've made a real breakthrough!"

"I have?" said the patient dubiously.

"Yes, Z," said the psychologist. He was thrilled, it was clear. "You *are* insignificant."

"I am?"

On the couch, Z's whole body sagged. How could he have been so stupid, so naive? How could he have thought, even for a minute, that he would find anybody who could truly understand his feelings? Especially this guy. Ant colonies didn't really have doctors who could understand someone like Z. Ant colonies had "motivational counselors." And they were just little cogs in the superorganism, exactly like him.

Sadly, his little antennas drooping, Z trudged back home to take his place among the worker ants on his detail. He didn't even look up at the mind-boggling enormousness of the tunnel. He didn't read the banner overhead, the one that read, THE MEGA-TUNNEL—TUNNELING OUR WAY TO A BRIGHT FUTURE! He had read it too many times before, and it always failed to inspire him.

In the gigantic tunnel, line after line of ants were working: digging, passing clumps of dirt from ant to ant, over and over again, every movement synchronized like a worker-ant ballet.

"Let's try it again," shouted the digging instructor. "Dig left, dig right, dig left, dig right, and again . . ."

Z sighed as he took his place in the line. "Okay," he said to himself, "I've got to keep a positive attitude, a good attitude, even though I'm utterly insignificant. I'm insignificant but with attitude."

A clump of dirt smacked him right in the face.

"Sorry, Z, I didn't see ya," said his friend Azteca, working away beside him. Azteca was very different from Z. She was a cheerful ant. A hearty ant. A happy little part of the superorganism.

"Great," said Z. "It's working already. I'm so meaningless I'm invisible."

He heaved his pick into the tunnel wall, and it immediately got stuck there.

Azteca moved over to help him out. "Now you're getting it," she said, easily wrenching the pick loose. "After all, it's not about you—it's about us, the team. It's about this." She swept her hand in a grand gesture that took in the whole gigantic Mega-Tunnel.

Z couldn't help smiling. "A giant hole in the ground?" he said.

Azteca just laughed. That Z. What a joker.

"Okay, people—are we feeling good?" yelled the foreman from farther down the digging line.

4

"Yeah!" shouted the workers, pumping their fists in the air.

"Yeah," said Z, trying hard.

"Great!" bellowed the foreman. "Now: R-1734 through Z-7829, you guys are on wrecking ball."

"You got it!" Azteca responded enthusiastically.

"Swell! You got it!" Z echoed her.

Immediately, Azteca, Z, and a big bunch of ants began clumping together. Pretty soon it was clear what they were doing: they were forming themselves into a big wrecking ball.

Z couldn't resist poking a little more fun at the whole business. "Now, remember, Azteca," he said wryly. " 'Be the ball!' That's the main thing here. Remember that, you gotta be one with the ball!"

Azteca laughed good-naturedly. "Cut it out already!" she said to her friend. "Geez, I love my work and you— well, you think too much! C'mon, Z. Help us build a bigger, better colony. And for crying out loud, try to be happy about it."

"Sure," said Z. "How could I possibly be unhappy about being a piece of construction equipment?"

The foreman was in high gear, revving his team. "Okay, workers, remember—"

Z winced. "Here it comes," he whispered to Azteca.

"Be the ball!" roared the foreman.

"Uuhhhgg," Z responded.

But his moan was drowned out by the chanting of a thousand happy workers: "Be the ball! Be the ball!"

"Grin and bear it," Z admonished himself. "This is for the colony."

The ball smashed into its target, a dirt column, destroying it in an explosion of dust.

Z flinched. "Oww, this is a lawsuit waiting to happen," he muttered.

"Hang on, here we go," said the worker above Z.

"Did I happen to mention that heights make me nauseous?" moaned Z.

Z tried, but he couldn't hang on. He lost his hold, and the whole wrecking ball fell apart as the foreman watched helplessly. The broken line of ants swung from the ceiling, with Z dangling from the end of it. Instead of "Be the ball," the motto could have been "Be in a state of mass confusion."

Z looked down at the milling swarm of ants below him. "I know, I know," he said to Azteca. "I dropped the ball."

Not long afterward, the same foreman stood in the middle of a large office, shivering with fear. General

Mandible, who was the iron commander of pretty much everything, stood with his back to the foreman, staring out a window. This was not a good sign, and the foreman knew it.

Nearby stood Colonel Cutter, Mandible's right-hand ant. Two guards stood at rigid attention by the door, making it clear that the foreman was not going to leave until Mandible was good and ready for him to go.

Mandible was brooding. "Workers," he muttered, as much to himself as to anybody else. "They're weak. They lack discipline. They lack commitment."

The foreman began to babble, terrified. "Sir," he blithered, "I know there's been a glitch or two, but everybody's working full tilt as it is, and—"

Mandible suddenly moved into the harsh light, and the foreman winced, expecting a blow.

"You can't help it," said Mandible in a tired voice. "It's your nature."

The foreman opened his eyes cautiously.

"But," Mandible continued, "in spite of your limitations, you *are* going to finish this tunnel. *On* schedule. Come hell or high water." The menace in his voice was clear now. He glanced over at Colonel Cutter, who looked ready to pounce at a word from Mandible.

"From now on," Mandible said to the foreman, "anyone who falls behind is going to have to personally explain themselves to Colonel Cutter. And let me assure you, the colonel is not as understanding as I am."

From the corner of his eye, the foreman could see Cutter responding with a quiet, predatory smile.

Mandible was through with the foreman. "Dismissed," he snapped.

After the foreman had been hustled out by the guards, Mandible turned to the colonel. "Four more days, Cutter," he said with barely suppressed excitement. "Four more days and we can bid final farewell to their kind of incompetence."

"Yes, sir."

"A fresh start. Imagine it."

"A stronger colony, sir, a colony we can be proud of."

"Yes, but we're not there yet," Mandible reminded him. He paused. "Cutter, we just got word that a termite army has mobilized against us."

"Against us?" Cutter said.

"We'll have to send troops deep into hostile territory to attack their colony," said Mandible grimly.

"Attack a termite colony? Sir—that's *suicide*!"

"Exactly," said Mandible. An evil little smile curled his lips. "Do you have the list I asked for?"

Cutter was beginning to catch on. He brought out a long list of names he had prepared. "Yes, General," he said, presenting the general with the list. "These are the units loyal to the Queen."

Mandible looked over the names. "Then they're the ones we'll be sending," he said. He looked pleased, very pleased. "It's a shame," he said. His voice was ice. "There are some fine officers here."

He handed the list back to Cutter. As usual, Cutter was regarding his boss with admiration for the genius, the deviousness, the sheer beauty of his mind. Here was an ant who would do whatever it took. Here was an ant who was rotten to the core.

Then he thought of something. He cleared his throat. "Don't we need the Queen's approval to declare war?" he asked delicately.

A brief grimace clouded Mandible's expression. "Our very next stop, Cutter," he said.

CHAPTER

In the Queen's chambers, Mandible and Cutter tried to ignore the fact that, as she conversed with them, their ruler was doing what queen ants do: she was having babies. Not just one or two babies—loads of babies. Cute little things, too. Even if they were impossible to tell apart.

As long as they had been in the Queen's court, this baby-having business was something they'd never quite gotten used to.

It certainly didn't bother the Queen. She simply kept talking.

"General," she was saying, "we've been at peace

with that termite colony for years. Why would they attack us?"

"They want our land. They're desperate for more foraging territory. Perhaps they think we've grown soft or weak."

"Why don't we dispatch an ambassador?" asked the Queen, having a baby. "Negotiate a new treaty? Certainly we don't need to send soldiers?"

A nurse came toward the Queen with a swaddled-up larva, and Mandible quickly stepped forward and took it from her instead, smiling sweetly.

Giving the baby a little pat, he handed it gently to Cutter. The colonel, who looked as though he'd been handed a live hand grenade, gave it back to the nurse as fast as possible.

"And that's why we must strike now," continued Mandible. "While we have the element of surprise. If the termite shock troops enter our colony . . . well . . ."

"Yes, General," said the Queen. "I know what they can do to us."

She weighed her decision, stopping to give her latest baby a quick cuddle. Finally, she sighed deeply. "Very well," she said unhappily.

"You've made a wise decision," said Mandible quickly. "In fact, you've ensured the future of this colony."

He saluted the Queen and turned to go.

As he did, a door opened from one of the ante-chambers, and in walked the lovely Princess Bala, heir to the Queen's throne. She walked with the assured, springy step of a high-spirited, smart princess who was accustomed to getting her way.

"Hello, General," she said.

Neither she nor the Queen could see his face, which was turned away. On it was an expression of furious frustration: he was going to be delayed. But when he turned smoothly to face Bala, he wore a pleasant smile.

"Princess Bala," he said smoothly. "What a nice surprise. You look lovelier each time I see you."

"Thanks," she replied.

Bala did not believe a word of his compliment. For a moment, she and Mandible stood there awkwardly, until finally the Queen coughed, looked pointedly at Bala, and then over to the general.

Bala moved closer to him. "I hope you're not just here on business," she said.

"No, of course not," he replied, trying to keep himself from glancing at the door.

"Because," she said, "it might be nice if we had a *conversation* once before we get married."

"You're absolutely right," said Mandible. "Cutter,

schedule some private time for me and Princess Bala." He began walking to the door.

"In fact, sir," Cutter interjected, "there's time right now for a personal moment. We're a few seconds ahead of schedule."

"Excellent," said Mandible heartily. "Princess?"

"Well," said Bala, "a few seconds isn't much, but . . . I guess if it's quality time . . ." She sighed, looked at her mother, and decided to make an effort. "So . . . how was your day? Did anything interesting happen?"

"We declared war," Mandible told her.

"Declared war?" she said. "Boy, talk about a rough day—"

"Sir, I hate to interrupt," said Cutter to the general, "but time stands still for no ant."

That was all Mandible needed to hear. "Princess," he said, ending the conversation. He clicked his heels and saluted. In a second, the general was out the door.

"Whew," she said, turning to the Queen after he'd gone. "Mom, could you remind me, why am I marrying this guy?"

The Queen was a bit distracted, juggling one baby while having another one. "Bala," she said, "do we have to argue about this again?"

"We just don't seem to have anything in common,"

Bala complained. "The guy's a stiff."

The Queen beckoned Bala to give her a hug, which was not easy, what with all the babies.

"Yes, darling, I know the general may be a little gruff and overbearing at times," she said, "but I know that he cares about you. He's just not particularly good at showing it. But you should have seen how *persistently* he asked for your hand in marriage."

"But why me?" wailed Bala.

The Queen made a sweeping gesture that took in the whole teeming ant nursery. "Because you're the one who has to continue my work. It's your place, dear."

"What if I don't like my place?"

"Everyone has their place, Bala. You, the soldiers, the workers. Now, it's not all *that* bad being a princess, is it? Would you prefer to be carting around dirt all day?"

"Oh, Mother. Don't be so dramatic."

The Princess crossed the room to the window and stood looking down at the colony, to where the workers' bar was. She could hear the faint strains of music floating up to her. "At least," she said wistfully, "*they* seem to have some fun now and then."

Inside that very bar, at that very moment, fun was indeed being had. All the way down the bar, which seemed to stretch for miles, rowdy ants were trying to get the attention of the lone bartender, a seasoned veteran who was slapping down what looked like large green beer mugs onto the bar as fast as he could. Actually, these things were aphids, little green critters that he filled up from a number of large kegs that hung from the ceiling. The kegs, in turn, were actually specialized ants with hugely swollen stomachs, who sprayed liquid into the aphids. Aphid beer was a big treat, if you were an ant.

Z was sitting at the bar with his friend Weaver, a burly but lovable soldier ant.

The bartender plunked down two of the green things in front of them. "Two aphid beers," he said.

The aphid beers did not seem to be lifting Z's mood. "Why'd I have to be born a worker?" he griped to Weaver. "You soldiers get all the glory. Plus you get to go out in the world—you know, you meet interesting insects, and you get to kill them."

"Yeah, but you get to spend all day with those beautiful worker girls," said Weaver, eyeing a group of them sitting at a table.

"Weaver, they're career girls. They're obsessed with digging." Z sighed. "I really don't think I'm ever gonna meet the right girl for me."

"Who said there *was* a girl for you?" Weaver grinned. "I was talking about a girl for *me*." He took a big swig of his drink. "Don't you want your aphid beer?" he said, yelling over the noise.

"Call me crazy," said Z, "but I have a thing about drinking from the rear end of another creature, OK?"

"Suit yourself. Me, I'm cutting loose. It's my last free night before royal inspection."

"Inspection. Meaning you're gonna stand around like an idiot while a bunch of blue bloods smirk at you. I don't know how you put up with it, Weaver."

Weaver put down his beer. "Z," he said, "I've known you for a long time, right?"

"Definitely. You were born two seconds after me."

"Yeah, and ever since we were little I've been listening to you complain. What're you whining about? In case you hadn't noticed, we ants are running the show. We're the lords of the earth!"

"Hey, don't talk to me about earth, OK?" grumbled Z. "I just spent all day hauling it around. There's just— there's got to be a better place."

A little way down the bar, there sat a grizzled old scout ant, nursing his umpteenth aphid beer. He was drunk; his head bobbed on his skinny neck. But he had heard what Z had said, every word of it.

16

"There *is* a place. I've been there," he said, staring straight ahead.

"I'm—I'm sorry—were you talking to me?" said Z.

The drunk turned to Z. "There *is* a better place. *Insectopia.*" His words were slurred but there was great intensity behind them.

The crowd around the bar was starting to back away from the scout, but Z was caught by his fierce gaze. He squirmed uncomfortably.

"Oh? Really?" he said, trying to edge away. He nudged Weaver in the thorax. "Lunatic at three o'clock," he whispered, rolling his eyes toward the old guy.

The drunk was really getting emotional now, his eyes riveting the unwilling Z. "You can't understand until you go there and see it for yourself!" he cried. "You can be your own ant there! The streets are paved with food! Nobody tellin' you what to do . . . no wars . . . no colony!"

The whole crowd gasped, shocked.

"I never shoulda left!" the scout said fervently.

Z was just trying to avoid eye contact with this weirdo. "Uh-huh. Fascinating," he mumbled.

The scout was a long way from finishing, though. "We were on a long-range recon," he said, deep into his combat flashback now. "I got cut off from my unit . . ."

17

Z nudged Weaver again. "Nothing like a little post-traumatic stress disorder to make your day complete," he cracked.

". . . and then I saw it," the old guy went on. "*Insectopia*. You head toward the monolith . . . ten clicks past the great canyons to the land of red and white . . ."

A group of soldiers who stood near him at the bar began to close in on him. "Hey, gramps," said one of them, putting an arm around his shoulders, "you've had enough for one night. C'mon before you get in trouble."

They pulled him from the bar and carried him out.

"Head for the monolith!" the scout shouted in Z's direction as he was dragged to the door. "Cross the lake . . . to the land of red and white . . ."

"That guy's got a screw loose," Weaver said to Z.

"Cross the lake!" the scout repeated. "Look for the land of red and white!"

Then he was gone and the sounds of the bar closed over the memory of the disturbance.

Z just stared down at the bar. "Insectopia. Wouldn't it be great if it were that easy."

"Yeah, dream on, Z," Weaver snorted.

CHAPTER

At that moment, at the entrance to the ant bar, three curious newcomers were peering inside. They had never been to a place like this before.

It was Princess Bala, accompanied by two worried-looking handmaidens.

"Wooowww," said the Princess, scanning the packed room. "This is so . . . gritty." It was clear from her rapt expression that she was hooked. There was no way she was not going in.

"Ten minutes and we're out of here, right?" fretted one of her handmaidens. "I mean, this place is off-limits."

Bala was hardly listening. "Look," she said, "just blame it on me. Say it was all my idea."

"It *is* all your idea," muttered the other handmaiden.

"Besides," Bala went on, unaware of her handmaiden's last remark, "no one's gonna recognize us. C'mon, girls, whaddya say? Let's take a walk on the wild side." She stepped inside the club.

Just then, the band began to play, and the place was filled with music. A barker took his place at a microphone at one end of the floor.

"Okay, everybody," he said into the mike. "It's six-fifteen, time to dance."

As one, the ants got up to dance, all at the same time.

Over at the bar, Weaver drained the last of his aphid beer. "Time to cut a rug, Z," he said, heading over to the dance floor.

Z stayed put. "Oh no, that's okay—I'm going to leave the rug just the way it is," he told Weaver.

"Suit yourself," said Weaver, shrugging. He went to join the rest of the ants who were lining up for the dance.

It was not exactly a wild and crazy scene. There at one end of the hall was the barker, calling out the steps in a bored monotone. And there on the dance floor were the ants, moving in perfect sync. The ants already knew all the steps.

From the door, Princess Bala and her handmaidens were watching the activity. There certainly wasn't anything like *this* at the palace. Bala was just itching to be part of the action.

"Step back, ladies," she said. "I'm gonna ask one of these workers to dance with me."

Z was leaning against the bar and watching, shaking his head. "What a bunch of losers," he said to nobody in particular. "Mindless zombies capitulating to an oppressive system."

"Hi. Wanna dance?" Bala had suddenly appeared before him.

It took about half a second for Z to totally abandon his principles. "Absolutely!" he replied. So much for the mindless zombies stuff.

He was smitten.

As they made their way onto the crowded floor, Z didn't break eye contact with Bala. He smiled suavely, or at least what he imagined to be suavely.

"So, uh—how come I haven't seen you around here before?" he asked as he followed her into the moving mass of ants. Above them a many-faceted fly eye served as the club's disco ball, casting dazzling pinpoints of light all over the room as it spun.

"I don't get out much. I work over at the palace."

"Oh, the palace, huh? I bet those royals really live it up." This was a subject Z could really warm to. "Of course they're all a little . . . *you* know . . . from inbreeding."

"*What?*" Bala was shocked.

They started dancing. Or trying to dance, in Z's case. He was not the Fred Astaire of the ant world, not by a long shot. In fact, he had six left feet. When everyone went left, he went right. When everybody went forward, he went back. Finally someone stepped on his toe, hard.

"*Yowch!*" he yelped.

But, since he didn't want his new love to think he was a total klutz, he quickly recovered. "*Yowch!*" he yelled again. He began clapping and *yowch*ing in time to the beat, hoping he could make it look as though he knew an extremely cool exclamation that was uttered while dancing. He tried to look as groovy as possible while clapping and *yowch*ing.

"What on earth are you doing?" Bala asked him.

Z had no choice but to tell the truth. "Well, actually, uh—to tell you the truth, I'm sort of making it up."

"Really?" Bala said, sounding intrigued.

"You know, why does everybody have to dance the same way? That's completely boring. It's, well, it's monotonous!"

"It's no fun!" Bala chimed in, totally won over.

Bala started to get into it, making up her own steps in reply to Z's made-up steps, loosening up and having fun. They were having a great time.

They were having *such* a great time, and they were so caught up in each other, that things started spinning a bit out of control. Their made-up dance got a little too wild. The other ants, who were still doing their perfect, intricate dance, started to collide with them.

"Hey! Watch your step, *worker!*"

Z spun around to find a soldier ant about twice his size towering over him menacingly.

Bala stuck her chin out. "You watch yours, buddy, or you'll be in *big trouble.*"

Maybe his partner didn't know enough to see her whole life flash before her eyes, but Z certainly did. Trembling, he stepped back. "That's, that's okay," he dithered, "I'm, I'm gonna let him off this time." Then he whispered to Bala, "Are you crazy? That guy's built like a *pebble!*"

"Aren't you even going to defend yourself?" demanded the indignant princess.

Z was caught between a rock and a hard place. He didn't want to get beaten up, but on the other hand, he didn't want to lose face in front of Bala.

Meanwhile, more of the gigantic soldier's gigantic

pals had gathered around, looking hostile.

"Hey, buddy," ordered one of them, "get back in place!"

"What if he doesn't want to?" retorted Bala.

Z rolled his eyes. She really was crazy. But she was so *beautiful*! He couldn't let her think he was a wimp. Better a dead brave guy than a live wimp.

Shaking with nervousness, he spoke to the soldier defiantly. "Yeah—what if I don't like my place?"

She smiled at him. Heaven. He smiled back.

"What's he talking about?" said a different gigantic soldier. The whole terrifying group began closing in threateningly.

"We got us a troublemaker!"

"Buckle up, Spanky. This one goes out to all the lazy workers!"

The first soldier threw a punch at Z, who was now praying to whoever he thought would listen.

SMACK! The soldier's huge hand was crushed against the great rippling abs of Weaver.

"You oughta watch that aggressive behavior, buddy," Weaver said evenly.

"He's just a worker!" said the outraged soldier.

The soldier then swung at Weaver, who ducked. But now Weaver was getting good and mad. He hoisted the

24

soldier up and threw him on to the bandstand. The band stopped playing as the soldier came crashing down on top of them. Almost immediately, disco music was piped in over the loudspeaker.

And so, to the cheery sounds of the bouncy music, havoc broke loose.

A soldier pushed Weaver, Weaver pushed him back, somebody made a dive for Z—and in the wink of an eye, there was a regular bar brawl going on.

Weaver was right in the middle of it, cracking heads together, punching ants in the face, and having a generally great time.

At the height of the mayhem, one of the Princess's handmaidens hurried over to her mistress. "Princess Bala! Princess Bala!" she cried. "The guards are coming!"

"Let's get out of here!" said Bala.

Z was at that moment on the floor under a very large and very drunk soldier. "Wait! *Princess?* You're a princess?" he said, trying to scramble out from under the soldier.

"Uh—I gotta go!" she said. She had to get out of there before the guards showed up!

"When can I see you again?" cried Z.

"Let me think. Hmmm . . ." She thought for about one second. "Never."

"No, wait!"

But Bala was out of there. The guards were getting closer, and that meant she was almost in big, big trouble. She bent down and gave Z a quick little peck on the cheek.

To Bala, this little kiss was nothing. But to Z, it was a life-changing experience. He watched, stricken with anguished adoration, as Bala rushed off through the brawling crowd with her handmaidens.

Instants later, the police descended on the place. Z just had time to see that Bala had gotten out safely before—

POW! Somebody punched him, but good. Lights out.

CHAPTER

The next day, despite a doozy of a headache, Z was back to his regular old worker-ant life, doing his regular old worker-ant things. But he was even less able to concentrate on his duties than usual. He was dreaming about his magical evening with Princess Bala and singing to himself. Every once in a while he'd even utter a nostalgic little "Yowch!," prompting his friend Azteca to wonder if he'd lost his mind.

Evening found him sitting in the bar again, dreaming, and hoping against hope that she'd show up. Now and then he'd cast a glance at the door. But things were pretty dead there tonight.

"Can I get you another one, pal?" said the bartender.

"No, thanks. I think I'm gonna go," said Z, standing up. It was late.

"Yeah, I don't blame ya," the bartender said as he mopped the bar with a rag. "It's always slow in here the night before one of those royal reviews."

Royal reviews.

Z was struck so swiftly by an idea, you could almost see it smack him. He reached the door before the bartender had even finished his thought.

"I guess the soldiers need their shuteye before they meet the Queen," the bartender went on. "Ya know, I was . . ."

Suddenly he realized he was talking to himself. Z was long gone.

In the soldiers' barracks, Weaver was slumbering peacefully. Suddenly, Z popped up beside him.

"Weaver! I figured it out!" he said, shaking the soldier. Weaver was out cold.

"WEAVER!" Z yelled in his ear. That did it. Weaver jolted awake.

"Weaver! I've got a great idea!" Z was so excited, he didn't even feel bad about waking up his friend.

"What?" said Weaver groggily.

"You've gotta switch places with me. Let me go to the inspection instead of you."

28

"What time is it?" Weaver was not with him yet.

"Weaver, the royal family will be there. This is the only way I can see her!"

"See who?"

"Princess Bala!"

"Are you nuts?" Weaver cried. "You want me to switch places with you?"

Weaver dropped his voice. The soldier ants in the cots nearby were starting to get interested in this dangerous conversation.

"Do you know how much trouble you can get in for even *talking* about impersonating a soldier?" Weaver asked Z in a low voice. "Heck, you could get in trouble for just *listening* to someone talking about impersonating a soldier!"

The eavesdropping ants turned away, covering their ears. Nobody wants trouble in an ant colony.

"You have to help me!" pleaded Z, having difficulty keeping his voice down. "If I can't see her again, my life is just not worth living! Please, please, please, Weaver, please! Switch with me just, you know, for a day! Think of all the things I've done for you!"

Weaver pondered briefly. "I can't think of any," he said.

Z thought fast. "Okay, so think of all the things that I'm *going* to do for you."

Weaver pondered once again. "Would I meet some

worker girls?" he asked.

"Are you kidding? They always go after the new guy, it's like sport for them. And believe me, they will definitely go for an adorable little insect like *you!*"

When Weaver looked doubtful, Z lapsed again into begging. "Weaver, I have to see her again!"

"Z, what kind of chance do you have with a princess?" Weaver asked him gently. "I mean, she probably won't even remember you."

"I know it sounds nuts, but I have to try."

Weaver could see that Z was just about at his wits' end. He took pity on him.

The royal review was a very grand affair. To the strains of heavy military music, with pennants flapping in the breeze, thousands of ant soldiers filled the streets of the town.

General Mandible stood on the reviewing stand, looking over the troops and slapping his thigh with a swagger stick. This was where he was at his best, where he really came alive: in front of an army of mindlessly obedient troops.

Z, buried in the ranks of Weaver's platoon, imitated the soldiers awkwardly as the army filed by in front of the royal reviewing stand.

Marching along with his platoon, Z practiced his casual little speech: "Princess! Fancy meeting you here. Hey, what do you say we lose this crowd? . . . Oh, me? I wear many hats. I guess you'd have to call me a Renaissance ant." As he babbled to himself he mimed tipping his army helmet to the Princess and smiling suavely.

Up on the reviewing stand, the Queen and Bala sat beside General Mandible, who had taken his place. As the troops filed past, Mandible saluted them.

"Beautiful! Just beautiful!" he murmured, right beside Bala's ear.

Bala started to smile. Maybe she had misjudged him. Maybe he had some romantic feelings after all.

"The precision," he continued, beaming with pleasure. "The order."

The smile on Bala's lips died. He'd been talking about the troops all along.

She rested her head on her hand, not even caring that she looked completely disinterested. Next to her, the Queen was giving the troops the little royal wave.

A tiny ant, just about lost in the sea of ants that stretched as far as the eye could see, was jumping up and down, waving frantically.

"Princess Bala! Princess Bala! Hey! It's me! From the

bar! Princess Bala, Princess Bala, Princess Bala!"

But Z was just a tiny speck to the princess, one of a zillion tiny specks. She couldn't distinguish him at all, couldn't hear what he was yelling. And she was hardly looking anyway. What did she care about reviewing the troops anyhow?

"Bala, you must encourage the troops," her mother admonished her. "Wave!"

Bala waved unenthusiastically, doing little more than flopping her hand back and forth on her wrist.

But down below, in the crowd, Z saw her wave and took this as a sign. She'd seen him! She'd seen him!

He began madly shoving his way toward her through the crowd. "She sees me! Excuse me. I just got a better offer. Could you let me through here, 'scuse me, fellas, I gotta—*unngh!*"

It just wasn't working. He was surrounded by a solid wall of soldiers. Big, big soldiers.

"Company, HALT!" boomed a loud voice.

Z wasn't interested in that particular idea. He was busy. His true love had waved. "Princess! Princess Bala!" he kept yelling.

"Quiet there! Get back in rank," he was ordered.

But Z was determinedly squeezing his way through the bodies.

The owner of one of the bodies tapped him on the shoulder.

Z looked up and found himself face to knees with a soldier about twice his size. The grunt looked hard as nails, like someone who had been through a lot of tough stuff—but he somehow had a kindly face, too. He looked down at Z and smiled.

"You new, kid?"

"Yes, yes," said Z, flustered. "But, you know, I'm getting out soon. I got a trial membership."

"Trial membership. That's a good one." The grunt chuckled. "Name's Barbatus," he said, extending his gigantic hand.

"Z," said Z, trying not to wince at the friendly hand-crushing.

The mass of soldiers stood in anticipation. General Mandible was going to speak. There was no point in Z's trying to make his way toward Bala now; he was thoroughly trapped.

"Right *face*!" The order floated over the crowd. Z, of course, made an immediate left face, bumping into Barbatus. Oops.

Mandible had stepped up to the microphone and was slapping his thigh with that stick again. Squinting at it, Z realized it was an antenna—probably the antenna of some unfortunate insect who had irritated the general.

There was a silence of several minutes while Mandible waited until the maximum dramatic effect had built up. Then he spat out one word.

"*Sacrifice.*"

He paused. He wanted it to sink in.

"To some," Mandible went on, "it is just a word. To others it is a *code.*"

"Geez," Z whispered to his large new friend. "You know, I'm really bad at word games."

Barbatus couldn't help but laugh a little. He liked this new guy. Even if he was a pip-squeak, he was a funny pip-squeak.

Mandible's voice boomed out over the troops. "A soldier knows," he continued, "that the life of an individual ant doesn't matter. What matters is the colony. He's willing to live for the colony. To fight for the colony. To *die* for the colony."

Z was still joking around. He wasn't quite picking up on where the general's speech was heading. "This guy's crazy," he mouthed to Barbatus.

"I hear ya," said Barbatus out of the corner of his mouth.

"At 0800 hours," said Mandible gravely, "we received word that the termite enemy has mobilized. We have no choice but to launch a preemptive strike. You are the

Queen's finest. I know you will all do your duty." He beamed. "I'm proud to send you into battle."

Suddenly, Z was listening. Suddenly, Z was scared. "Into, I'm sorry, I'm sorry—into battle?" he gibbered, his teeth chattering.

Up on the podium, Mandible clicked his heels smartly. "Dis-*missed*," he barked to the troops.

With another cheer, the troops started moving.

This was it. They were on the march. They were going to war. Z was swept along with the mass of ants, out of the colony and up into the night. How had this happened? Z was out of his wits with fear, but there was no getting out of it now. He was trapped. There were a zillion soldiers in every direction, all marching in lockstep.

"You know, I think there's been a terrible mistake!" he babbled to anyone who would listen. "I, you know, the truth is I just came for the speech . . ."

"Don't worry, kid, I'll watch out for you," said Barbatus, taking pity on him. Poor little guy. He sure didn't seem like a regular sort of soldier.

CHAPTER

All around Z and Barbatus, the army of ants started up a marching song.

"Sound off!"

"One! Two!"

"Sound off!"

"Three—"

"—Huh?" It was Z's turn to sound off. He wasn't getting the hang of this.

The song continued: "We ants go marching one by one, hurrah, hurrah! We slaughter termites just for fun, hurrah, hurrah!"

Somehow the song was not making Z feel any better. "So," he said to Barbatus, "these termites, they're not going to put up much of a fight, right? I mean, we're talking about pushovers, right?"

Barbatus smiled grimly. "Not really, kid. They're five times our size, and they shoot acid from their foreheads."

This stopped Z right in his tracks. What had he gotten himself into?

The soldier behind Z crashed right into him. "Ooof! Hey, keep it moving, shorty!" he snapped.

The ants were still singing: "We ants go marching two by two. Hurrah! Hurrah! We'll all be dead before we're through. Hurrah! Hurrah!"

Z was feeling queasy. He nudged Barbatus again. "Uh, say, what exactly does our platoon do? I mean, are we gonna be serving beverages? Processing paperwork?"

"Our platoon has the best assignment of all," Barbatus told Z, his voice brimming with pride. "We're the first into battle!"

". . . We ants are marching three by three. Hurrah! Hurrah! We're off to face our destiny. Hurrah! Hurrah!"

"Hey! Wait a minute, let's not get—we're being too hasty here!" yelled Z over the singing. "These—these guys sound like bruisers. I mean, just how were you figuring on beating them?"

"Superior numbers, kid," Barbatus explained patiently. "We overwhelm their defenses and kill their queen."

Z was shocked. "Aren't you being a little extreme? Why don't we just try to influence their political process with campaign contributions?"

Barbatus laughed. "I like you, kid. You got a sense of humor."

An order was shrieked from the front of the ant army: "Foooooorrrwwaaaaarrddd!"

"Come on, kid, let's kick some termite butt." Barbatus chuckled again, but it was a pretty grim chuckle.

Looming straight ahead of them was the termite colony. It was built in the stump of a dead tree, and it looked to Z like some kind of demonic mountain. There was no way he could imagine going over the top.

"OVER THE TOOOPP!!" shouted Barbatus.

The ant army swarmed straight toward the termite colony, up the side of the stump, and over the top, sweeping Z along with it. Ants were everywhere, engulfing the tree stump inside and out. They were ready to take on their fearsome enemy. They were ready to fight . . .

. . . what? It was completely deserted inside. It was peaceful. It was termiteless.

"Where is everyone?" the ants started asking each other.

"What's going on?"

"Something's not right."

There was a strange tapping noise. *Tap-tap. Tappa-tappa-tap-tap-tap*.

Everyone looked around to find the source of the noise.

It was Z's teeth chattering in fear.

Then there was something else. It wasn't a sound. It was more like a feeling—a feeling of being watched. As their eyes grew accustomed to the pitch-blackness inside the stump, the ants began to make out thousands of holes chewed into the inner walls of the stump. Termite holes. With termites in them.

"Don't be scared, kid," said Barbatus.

And then the termites were upon them. Before there was time to think, before there was time to react, they were in the middle of a massacre. The ants had broken into the colony, but they did not have the advantage of surprise. They were already taking heavy losses from the gigantic, blind, acid-spewing termites.

The battle scene was chaotic. Both sides were taking losses. A squad of ants rushed toward a termite soldier, but they were melted into smoking heaps of flesh by a jet of acid from the termite's forehead. Nearby, a termite warrior was overwhelmed by a crowd of ants and pulled to pieces with hideous ripping sounds. Ant soldiers were having their heads slowly crushed by huge termite jaws.

It was a hideous nightmare. Z wanted nothing more than to get out of this dreadful place. But just then, a termite burst up from the ground and turned to face him.

Z was dwarfed by this hulking, roaring, drooling monstrosity. The termite reared, getting ready to melt Z with its terrifying acid, when—*Oof*! It was knocked backward by Barbatus.

Z was overwhelmed. "Barbatus, you saved my life!" he panted, hugging his friend around the abdomen.

"Don't get all sappy about it!" said Barbatus.

There wasn't time to get sappy anyhow. There was only time to keep fighting. Z and Barbatus, back to back, turned to face the battle.

An ant was in trouble nearby, and Barbatus ran off to help. Z just stood there, not knowing what to do next.

A little way off, he saw a termite rising up behind a group of soldiers, drooling acid. The soldiers were busy polishing off a termite that had just tried to kill them, and they didn't yet see the danger from the rear.

"Hey, guys, look out behind you!" yelled Z.

But his attempt to help his fellow soldiers backfired. The termite wheeled to face Z, then began to chase him.

Z ran. As he did, he fell into a hole in the ground, escaping the shooting acid of the termite by a hair's-breadth.

"Whew!" he puffed, safe for the moment in his hole. He looked out on the horrific battle, wishing he were anyplace else but here.

CRASH!

The termite was felled by the ants. Its lifeless body toppled to the ground in a shower of spewing acid and came to rest with an earth-shaking thud right in front of Z's hole. The termite's body shielded Z from its own acid and kept him safe from the roaring battle outside.

The next thing Z knew, it was morning. The battle was over. Z made his way across the corpse-strewn battlefield. His face showed the horror he was feeling.

"Kid? Kid! Over here," said a weak but familiar voice.

"Barbatus?" said Z hopefully.

Z followed the voice, picking his way over the bodies. There. There he was.

Z's heart sank. It was Barbatus, but it wasn't all of him. It was just his head.

"Be honest, kid—am I hurt bad?"

Z tried to lie, but he was not good at it. "No, no, not at all, you're, you're, actually you're . . . lookin'—terrific. You've got, you know, swell color in your cheeks." He

41

choked back a sob.

"No—I can see it in your eyes. I'm a goner. Help me up, Z."

Z tried to lift Barbatus's head up a little. Barbatus winced. "Ooh . . . I can't feel my legs . . ."

"You gotta hang in there, buddy!" Z urged him desperately. "I know you're gonna make it! Just take—take deep breaths, 'cause I'm, I'm gonna, I'm gonna try and find your body. It's bound to be out there somewhere!"

Helplessly, Z scanned the battlefield, trying to distinguish Barbatus's body parts from the others that were strewn in tangled profusion nearby. Barbatus coughed.

"Barbatus? Hang, hang on!"

But Barbatus had something to tell Z, something important. He knew he was going. "Kid," he whispered.

Z ran back to his friend and leaned down to hear him.

"Don't make my mistake, kid," said the soldier. He coughed painfully. "Don't follow orders your whole life. Think for yourself."

"Barbatus!" cried Z, trying to keep his friend from slipping away.

But the brave soldier was gone, leaving Z with only his last words and a broken heart.

CHAPTER

Meanwhile, life was going in a perfectly normal way back in the Mega-Tunnel. There were no wars here, just the constant battle between ant and dirt.

In Z's place, working with great zeal, was his friend Weaver. Even though he was much larger than the others, he was managing to pass as a worker.

Weaver had found, to his surprise, that he actually loved the work. Wind up and—*Wham!* Wind up—*Wham!* He was wielding his pickax like a powerful digging machine. He loved the rhythm. He loved pitting his muscle against the unflinching rock of the wall. This was great!

Beside him, Azteca was working at her usual steady

pace. But when she noticed Weaver going crazy next to her, she stopped to watch for a minute. This guy was something else.

Weaver went into overdrive, really getting into it now. "Oh, yeah, big guy comin' through!" he sang out. "Love it!"

When they had cleared that section of the tunnel, it was time for a break. Azteca leaned on her shovel. "Hey, take it easy, Muscles," she said to Weaver, in a voice that made him think of smoke and velvet. "You're making the rest of us look bad!" She gave him a flirty smile. He gave her one back.

Suddenly she had a thought. "Hey," she said, "what happened to Z?"

"Um, he's taking a personal day, so I'm filling in."

"You fill in any more and you'll explode," she said admiringly.

Weaver was hardly listening anymore. He was checking out Azteca's legs. All of them.

Azteca waved her hand in front of Weaver's face and drew his gaze back up to her face, where it was supposed to be. "Hey, ya gotta problem?" she said.

"No," he said, recovering. "Uh, nobody told me digging was so much fun! You know, you pick the dirt up, you move it, you pick it up again, you move it again—

lots of reps, you exercise the arms and the thorax . . ."

Azteca couldn't help ogling him. "Hmm, yes, I see what you mean . . ."

The two of them were so entranced with each other they hadn't noticed that work had started again. Clods of earth were piling up behind Weaver.

The foreman came striding down the line. Nobody liked him. He was the type of guy who acts like he's your friend one minute, and turns on you the next.

"Yeah," he said sarcastically to Weaver, "that is fascinating!"

Weaver, forgetting he wasn't in the army, whipped his shovel up to his shoulder and saluted.

"Sorry, sir," he said, as if he were addressing a superior officer. "I was just having a little chat with my friend—*sir!*"

"Well, I just had a little chat with General Mandible," said the foreman nastily. "He informed me that anybody who doesn't meet his quota is going to be ... downsized."

Azteca stepped right up to the foreman's face. "Hey, cut him a break! He's new!" she said.

Now the foreman was mad. "Hey! What do you say we help your attitude a little bit by taking away your rations for the day?" He sneered, pleased with himself.

"Thanks for your time," he added as he moved down the line.

Azteca went back to work, digging furiously. She was surprised at herself. "I don't know what came over me," she said, more to herself than anybody else, "talking back like that. I must be losin' it . . ."

Weaver leaned over to her, dodging her pickax, which she was now swinging feverishly. She was not trying to miss him, either. "Sorry I got you in trouble," he said.

Wham!

"But, listen, you can—"

Wham!

"—share my rations if you want."

Azteca's pick swung in Weaver's direction again. But this time he blocked her pick with his own. She stopped swinging.

"Are you asking me out to dinner?" she asked him, waving her feelers fetchingly.

Weaver blushed. "Well . . . if you don't have anything else planned . . ."

"I'll check my calendar. " She giggled. "You know, I'm kinda glad Z's taking a breather."

In General Mandible's chambers, Mandible and Cutter

were studying a diagram of the completed Mega-Tunnel.

"We're on schedule," Cutter reported. "Work is completed on A-section, sir, and we're clearing a path through D-section now."

"We need to push harder, Cutter. I want double shifts, round the clock, seven days a week. We can't afford to let up. Is that clear?"

"Crystal, sir," said Cutter.

"Good," Mandible snapped. "Now, what about section G?"

There was a hesitant tap on the open door, and an officer timidly entered the room. "Excuse me, sir," he said.

"This had better be important!" roared Mandible.

The officer was afraid to raise his eyes from the floor. "Sir . . . the attack on the termites. . . I'm afraid it was a disaster."

"Oh? That's terrible. Terrible!" Mandible hardly bothered to conceal his glee.

"There is a bit of good news, sir," the officer reported. "One soldier did make it back."

"*What did you say?*"

"Word is spreading through the colony, sir," said the officer. "The Queen has requested a meeting with the war hero."

"Darn—" the general began, clearly annoyed. Then, remembering the officer, he quickly added, "—good. Darn good. I'll take care of it." He dismissed the officer.

Mandible paced the room. Darn right he'd take care of this. Who was this upstart? Probably some big brainless lug who wanted to be a star. He'd messed up Mandible's perfect plan—and Mandible would make him pay. But he'd have to be careful about it. After all, he was dealing with a war hero.

There was already an escort assembled for the new hero, and they were all gathered in the hallway outside the throne room. Mandible strode into the group, immediately taking charge. He almost missed Z, who was dwarfed by his military companions.

"Congratulations, soldier," Mandible said to the large, burly soldier next to Z. Then, realizing his mistake, he looked down at the top of Z's head. "You're a little short for a war hero, aren't you?"

Z was still traumatized. He could barely understand what was going on. What was he doing here? Who were these people? Why was he still alive? "War hero?" he said falteringly. "Sir, I . . . I actually don't think that I'm a hero—"

"Good," said Mandible quickly. "I don't like heroes."

Z was hustled down the hall and out onto a balcony that overlooked the great town square. A crowd was already assembled there to greet the conquering hero. When Z and the others stepped out into the light, the crowd roared. Z could just make out a banner being waved below that said, ONE TO NOTHING, WE WIN.

This was all too much for him. Not long ago, he had been in the middle of a scene of unimaginable carnage. He had watched thousands of good ants die, and to one of them he owed his life. He turned to Mandible, who was waving amiably to the crowd.

"But, you don't understand," he said, half to himself. "I didn't do anything. I mean, it was horrible, it was just a massacre. A massacre upon a massa—"

"That's good, soldier," Mandible interrupted him, still pleasant but with just a bit more edge. "Now *wave.*"

Down below, in the jam-packed streets, Weaver and Azteca were making their way to the town square. Weaver was upset, walking fast, trying to get through the people at the edge of the crowd.

"I just feel horrible," he said to Azteca. "Poor Z, I should have never let him go."

Azteca squinted at the waving figures, and as she did, her expression changed.

"Wait a minute," she said, grabbing Weaver's arm. "That's no soldier—that's Z!"

Weaver's mouth fell open. "Z?! The little guy made it!"

CHAPTER

Up on the balcony, Z was going with the flow. Mandible raised his arms, the crowd cheered. Z raised his arms, the crowd cheered. He did it again, they did it again. It was like a game.

Then, abruptly, the game was over. "Let's go, soldier," said Mandible. He motioned to the escort, and Z was whisked off the balcony.

There was no time to dawdle. They were expected in the throne room for Z's audience with the Queen. They hustled down the hall to where the huge, heavy doors were thrown open to reveal the whole royal entourage, waiting impatiently for the returning hero.

Mandible lost no time in playing to the crowd. He was the great conquering general and loyal servant of the Queen. Meanwhile, Z was looking around, taking in the opulent setting.

"As I was saying," the general said to Z as they stepped onto the red carpet that led to the throne, "you are an ant after my own heart. An ant that looks death in the face and laughs."

"Actually, the truth is," Z replied, "I generally just make belittling comments and snicker behind death's back."

They had almost reached the throne. "Keep your comments to yourself. Let me do the talking," warned the general.

And then, there Z was, not a feeler's distance away from her: Princess Bala. She stood next to the Queen. She looked as beautiful as he remembered her from the bar. More beautiful, even.

Mandible bowed deeply to the Queen. "May I present her majesty the Queen—"

"Charmed, charmed," blithered Z, much too star-struck to have any manners at all.

"—and the Royal Princess Bala," the general continued.

Z had gone way beyond stupid. He gave Bala what he thought of as a sexy sort of growl. The Queen simply ignored it.

"Welcome home, soldier," she said. "We cannot begin

to express our gratitude for your heroic efforts."

Mandible hastily answered before Z could open his mouth: "The private has asked me to convey his most humble appreciation for this honor."

But Z was not able to keep his mouth shut, not even in the face of Mandible's undisguised glare. He was desperate to impress the Princess. "Please, please, it was nothing really, just your average, run-of-the-mill valor and extraordinary courageousness. You know, in the heat of battle, there's very little time to think. One must attack! Attack! Attack!"

He threw out his arms in a sweeping gesture and knocked a tray out of a nearby waiter's hand. It fell to the ground with a clatter, and the flustered Z dove for the mess, frantically picking up canapés and cutlery. Some war hero.

"Indeed," said the general, disgusted. He had to get this yo-yo out of there before he did something *really* stupid. "Well, as you can see, Your Highness, the battlefield is still fresh in his mind. So, begging your pardon, but I think this is the perfect time to debrief the private."

"Please, General—not on our first date!" Z tried to laugh nonchalantly, but the joke fell as flat as a wet leaf.

But something about that particular stupid joke jogged the Princess's memory. A flash of recognition traveled across her face. "Hey, haven't I seen you somewhere before?" she said to Z.

Z froze, unsure what to say. "Maybe. Then again, maybe not. Then again—" Oh, what the heck. He gave her a nudge and a broad wink. "*Yowch!*" he said.

"That's it—you're the guy from the bar!"

"Shhhh!" said Z. Now she was going to get them both in big trouble.

Bala, as usual, was too excited to be careful. "I danced with this guy at the bar the other night," she told her mother. Then she remembered something. "But—he was just a worker then!"

The Queen was not interested in Z at that moment. "What were you doing at a bar?" she wanted to know.

"Precisely what I want to know!" barked a furious Mandible.

Bala had to think fast. "No," she said excitedly. "This isn't about me," she continued, trying to divert their attention. "I mean, look at this worker—look what he's done!"

Now Z was really nervous. "I think you're thinking about someone else. After all, I am a soldier." He tried to will her to shut up.

No such luck. Bala was thrilled. "Exactly! You *were* a worker, but now—you're a war hero!"

"He's a worker?" said the astonished Queen.

"A worker danced with my fiancée?" said the outraged Mandible.

Suddenly, in about two seconds flat, Z had gone from a war hero to a jerk.

"Fi-fi-fiancée?" This was big news to Z. Big, scary news. "W-wait a minute—it's not how it looks, I can explain . . ." Now the war hero chickened out completely. "Hey, she was the one making all the moves!" he said, gesturing toward Bala.

The general started moving threateningly toward Z. "Arrest him!" he ordered.

Z began backing away from Mandible. "Hey, wait a minute, take it easy, can't we discuss this?" he said. Still backing away from the general, he bumped smack into Bala. He grabbed hold of her to steady himself.

"What are you doing?" screamed the Queen. "Let go of my daughter!" She was getting hysterical now. Her baby! "He's taking her hostage!" she screeched.

"No, I'm not!" Z protested. Then he changed his mind, realizing she was his only ticket to getting out of this alive. "I mean—yes, I am!" He tightened his grip on Bala, who struggled mightily.

"One more step and the Princess gets it!" Z threatened, snatching up a canapé and holding the toothpick to her throat. He had not a clue what she would get, naturally.

Meanwhile, Bala, with her free hand, was bopping him repeatedly over the head. "Let go of me!" she yelled.

Still struggling, Z and Bala lurched across the throne room and fell headlong into a garbage chute.

There was no time to think as the two of them hurtled down the long chute. Along the way, they crashed into all manner of disgusting stuff and just kept bumping and bashing and slithering their way down . . .

And out.

Screaming, Bala and Z flew through the air, finally hitting the ground with a great thump. They bounced like rubber balls through a hollow log and shot out once again, this time into a slimy pool of rotting leaves and twigs, where they finally came to a stop. They were out in the wilderness.

Bala was boiling mad. "What are you doing, you creep? Are you out of your puny little mind?" she yelled at Z. She did not appear to share the warm and fuzzy feeling that Z had carried away with him from the bar that night.

They heard Mandible's soldiers behind them, in pursuit: "There they are, down there! Let's go! Move, move, move!"

"Oh, good," said Bala, "here they come to rescue me and kill you!"

"*Kill?*" yelped Z. How had they gotten to *kill?* A minute ago he'd been a hero!

Bala started waving her arms madly, trying to get the soldiers' attention. "Hey, you guys!" she called.

"Stop it! What are you trying to do?" whispered Z. He tried to stop her from waving but only succeeded in getting inadvertently smacked in the face.

"Ow! Hey, get out of my way, you little twerp!" she snapped at him.

"Wait a minute. Do you want to throw away everything we've got?"

Bala ignored him and continued waving to the soldiers. "What are you waiting for? Hello! Guys!" She started running toward the soldiers.

But Z wasn't looking at her at that moment. Neither were the soldiers. They were all looking at something huge that hovered overhead. None of them had ever seen anything like it. It was beautiful—a giant, clear disk, rimmed with metal.

Bala stopped running as the huge shadow of the hovering thing passed over her. The soldiers stopped too.

And then, skimming across the ground, came a shaft of brilliant light, which seemed to be emanating from the clear disk. It was brighter than anything the ants had ever seen. It was dazzling, like a pillar of the purest white fire.

"What is it?" said one of the soldiers. "It's beautiful!"

"Ridgeway, get outta there!" shouted the soldier behind him. But it was too late. The sizzling beam flashed out from the disk, coming to rest on Ridgeway, focusing all the power of the sun on one tiny ant.

He screamed for a moment, and then he was gone, incinerated, a smoking pile of ex-ant. Then the giant glass disk moved on.

Bala and Z were already sprinting for cover, zigzagging across the clearing, as the death ray swept across the platoon of guard ants, burning them all up in a split second. Panting, Bala and Z took shelter in the huge shadow of a pebble. "Whew! Safe!" gasped Z.

But this was not true. The giant disk was still seeking them. As Bala and Z trembled, their sheltering rock was lifted up with an earth-shaking rumble. The disk, like some malevolent entity, craned around the rock, looking for the two stragglers.

They couldn't stay there, clearly. They started running again, staying just ahead of the demolishing beam.

Suddenly, Z screeched to a halt, just in time to keep himself from hurtling headlong off the edge of a cliff. But Bala was unable to stop herself. She crashed into Z, and together they plummeted, down and down in a bumpy descent to the ground below, where they slid

"There *is* a better place. Insectopia."

Bala and Z cut a rug on the dance floor.

"Please, switch places with me." Z begs Weaver to let him join the army for the Queen's inspection.

"Big guy coming through!" Weaver takes Z's place as a worker.

General Mandible announces his plan to attack the termite colony.

Z narrowly escapes the vicious, acid-spewing termites.

"Please, switch places with me." Z begs Weaver to let him join the army for the Queen's inspection.

"Big guy coming through!" Weaver takes Z's place as a worker.

General Mandible announces his plan to attack the termite colony.

Z narrowly escapes the vicious, acid-spewing termites.

"What are you doing, you creep?" Z kidnaps Princess Bala and drags her into the wilderness.

"Hold on, I'll get you out!" Bala yells.

"Let's eat!"

Z struggles to break through the "force field."

"Excuse me . . . this is a private function,"
Chip tells the intruders.

A sticky situation for Bala and Z.

The Monolith.

Bala and Z prepare to make their way across the lake.

At last, they find it—Insectopia.

That was it. Nobody was digging. They were all talking about the Legend of Z.

The foreman strode into the group, having finally gotten word of what was happening. "People, people! What is this, an encounter group? Get back to work."

"Why?" somebody wanted to know.

"We don't have to work on the tunnel anymore!" yelled someone else. "Z's leading a revolution!"

This was not the sort of problem the foreman had ever run into before. Incompetent workers, yes. Loafing on the job, sure. But a revolution? What was he supposed to do with this?

He backed away. "I'll, um, get back to you," he said.

At that moment, the unwitting leader of the revolution and his unwilling companion were trudging along in a vast, glimmering desert wasteland. They were just two tiny dots moving across the endless arid whiteness. Every once in a while, a gigantic machine of some sort, thundering along on two enormous wheels, would rumble past them. They were getting used to this; it was just one more huge, terrifying thing in a new world full of huge, terrifying things.

"Think about it, Z," Bala was saying. "Two ants. Who ever heard of two ants? Two *million* ants, maybe—but two?" She stopped trudging and rubbed a couple of her feet. "Look, I'm hungry. I'm thirsty. And this whole desert thing, it just doesn't work for me." She rubbed another foot gingerly. "I think," she said, "it's about time for you to take me back."

Z stopped and gave her a baleful look. "Take yourself back," he said grouchily. Then he started walking again.

"*Excuse* me," she said, running to catch up with him. "You kidnapped me, remember? That means you have certain responsibilities! You can't just abandon me here in the wilderness!"

Z was in no mood. "It's better than being back at the colony," he said.

"You're not serious, are you?"

"Maybe you were living the high life, but personally, I'd say this beats digging. If you'd ever done a day's labor, you'd know what I was talking about." He plunged ahead of her again.

"Labor?" she yelled, catching up again. "What do you know about labor? How would you feel if you were expected to give birth every ten seconds for the rest of your life?"

"Hmmm," he said. This was a new concept for him, he had to admit.

Bala, however, wasn't even interested in his reaction,

because she'd seen something—something marvelous. Water! Real live water!

She brushed past him in her rush to get to the glittering lake. But she couldn't resist one last dig. "All you think about is yourself!" she yelled back to him.

"Yeah, well, nobody else ever thought about me," he said as he hustled to keep up with her. "So as far as I'm concerned, I don't need anybody else."

The lake was filled to the brim with wet, delicious water. They started lapping it up thirstily.

What they did not know was that there was a towering stone structure in the middle of the lake. Just then, a big drop of water was trembling on the edge of it. Suddenly . . . *CRASH!* Like a giant bomb, the water drop splashed down, down into the lake.

The huge drop sent many smaller drops flying into the air. Bala scrambled to safety, but Z didn't make it. One of the drops completely engulfed him. The drop— with Z inside—landed on top of a small hill.

"Bala! Help me, Bala!" he screamed, his voice muffled by the sphere of water in which he was trapped. He jumped up and down, holding his breath. But the droplet, held firm by surface tension, would not burst. It just sort of quivered up and down. Z was slowly, frantically drowning.

"Hold on, I'll get you out. Hold on!" Bala yelled, scrambling up the side of the hill. She found a stick and started hitting the bubble with it, smashing Z over the head in the process. But the bubble wouldn't break.

Bala didn't give up, though. She kept on bashing the bubble, until, with a tremendous effort, she suddenly found herself inside the bubble too.

Now they were both struggling and screaming. But it turned out that struggling and screaming was a good plan, because all the movement sent the water droplet over the edge. It smashed onto the rocks below, and burst. Z and Bala lay there, soaked and panting.

"Thanks," he gasped.

"Don't mention it," she said with a wry little laugh. She was surprised at herself. As a princess, she was used to having others help her. This was the first time she had ever actually helped anyone else, and it felt kind of good.

"Now maybe we can put this fantasy behind us and head back to the colo—" She stopped dead, right in the middle of the sentence, and they looked at each other. For a moment, they gazed deep into each other's eyes.

Then Z turned away, feeling a little self-conscious. He busied himself by starting to drag a leaf to the edge of the water.

"Uh . . . Z? What are you doing?"

"We've got to cross the lake," he said, full of determination.

"Am I missing something here? Didn't we just get *out* of the water?"

He turned to look at her. "Bala, look—what have you got to lose? I mean, think about it. Do you really want to be Mrs. Raving Lunatic?"

She couldn't help herself. She smiled.

"There's a better place," he said to her. "Just give me one chance. If we don't find Insectopia soon, I promise I'll take you back to the colony."

Bala thought for a moment. Then she took Z's hand and stepped onto the leaf. "I hope I don't regret this," she said.

The leaf started drifting across the water. "Don't worry," said Z. Then he went into a pretty good imitation of Mandible. "Bala, you're an ant after my own heart, an ant that looks death in the face and laughs . . ."

"Cut it out!" Bala giggled, in spite of herself.

Mandible stood in the Mega-Tunnel, frowning. He was observing a group of workers who had stopped work and were sitting down, chanting.

"Z! Z! Z! Z!" they went. More and more workers were throwing down their tools and joining them in the sit-down strike.

The foreman was exhorting them, totally ineffectually: "People! Come on! I know some ants who aren't gonna make their quota!"

"Buzz off, pawn of the oppressor!" somebody cat-called.

"We want Z! We want Z! We want Z!" went the new chant.

In another part of the room, the ants began to sing something about giving Z a chance.

Mandible shuddered in horror as Cutter hurried up to him.

"Sorry, sir," said Cutter. "I came as soon as I heard. I was debriefing the trackers."

"And, what's the report?"

Cutter was nervous. "Well, this 'Z,' sir, is one slippery character; they lost Bala's trail at the edge of the lake—"

"The lake?" Mandible shouted. The word had stopped him in his tracks.

Then he noticed something else. He noticed a soldier ant—right in the middle of all the worker ants. It was Weaver, standing with Azteca.

"What's that soldier doing there?" Mandible barked at Cutter.

Cutter looked at Weaver. "It appears he's holding hands, sir. With a worker."

Mandible's eyes narrowed. "I don't like the way things are going, Cutter. I am counting on you for results. Now, can I depend on you or not?"

"Yes, sir."

Mandible resumed his march down the tunnel, now with more urgency. Cutter struggled to keep up with the larger ant.

"All right then. Let's wrap this up," Mandible said.

Down in the pit, at the center of the group, Weaver and Azteca were holding hands, leading the workers in song. "All we are saying . . ." they sang.

Mandible stepped to the front of the crowd of strikers. He was good at speaking to large groups.

"I've heard a lot about this 'Z,'" he shouted, in his most commanding voice.

There were a few more random "Z!" chants from the crowd.

"I even had the pleasure of meeting him once," the general continued. The crowd began to pay attention. "BUT WHERE IS HE NOW?" continued the general, gathering a good head of steam. "Can anyone point him out?" He paused, just long enough for maximum effect. "I mean, if this Z cares so much about us, then why isn't he here?"

The crowd began to look confused.

"I'll tell you why," said Mandible, answering his own question. "It's because Z doesn't give a darn about us!"

To this accusation, nobody in the crowd had an answer.

Mandible was really rolling now. "That's why he kidnapped our princess! That's why he ran away!" There was some nodding in agreement and grumbling going around the crowd now, but Mandible wasn't finished. "Z is no hero! *We* are the heroes. We're the ones ensuring the future of our great colony. And when we've completed this magnificent structure, we will reap the benefits."

The crowd was now cheering as he went into his magnificent wrap-up.

"More food for everyone! More rest as a reward for our honest efforts! And each and every one of you will get the day off so that you can be *the* guest of honor at the Mega-Tunnel Dedication Ceremonies!"

The crowd erupted into even wilder cheering, and the foreman, who wasn't totally stupid, saw his chance to make something out of it. "Man-di-ble!" he started chanting loudly. "Man-di-ble!"

The workers, whipped up into a mindless lather, immediately took up the chant. "MAN-DI-BLE! MAN-DI-BLE! MAN-DI-BLE!"

Mandible threw his hands up in the air like the brilliant political operator he was. Then he marched out, a startled Cutter in tow.

Unbelievable. The whole performance had been unbelievable. Cutter shook his head.

"Now," Mandible said quietly, leaning over to Cutter, "bring me that soldier."

He pointed straight at Weaver.

CHAPTER

Out in the wilderness, Bala was waking up. Z was still sleeping beside her. Well, almost beside her. She had propped a leaf in between them, so Z wouldn't try anything funny.

She sat up, getting her bearings. Then she decided to go exploring. She moseyed around a bit through the weeds, parted two blades of grass, and—

"Oh my God, Z, c'mere!"

She was staring at something that loomed up in the distance. It was a monumental structure—a huge red-and-blue cylinder that towered over the landscape. It had to be the Monolith.

Z was up now, standing beside her and rubbing his eyes. "It's Insectopia!" he cried.

"My God, you were right, it really is here!" said Bala.

"Eh?" he said, pretending he couldn't hear her. He had to make her suffer a *little* for doubting him, didn't he?

"All right, all right, you're a genius!" she said.

Food! And loads of it, all arranged on an endless landscape of red and white squares, just there for the taking—the land of red and white, exactly as the old scout had said. Z and Bala made a beeline, or rather an antline, for the promised land.

Wowee! Big white squares of soft flat stuff! With other stuff in the middle! Z immediately started to dig in. Insectopia! This was the life!

But something was wrong. The white-things-with-stuff-in-between were protected in some way, by a thin layer of shiny clear stuff. Z hurled himself at the layer, bopped it, tried to chew through it . . . but no luck. It was impregnable.

"Well? What's the problem? I'm hungry!" said Bala.

"There's some kind of force field!" yelled Z, desperately banging at it. There was the wonderful food—he could smell it! But he couldn't get past the force field.

There was a loud, loud droning sound in the air

above them, and a shadow fell across the ground in front of Z. It was a wasp, a male. Maybe the wasp knew how to get through this force field. "Excuse me," Z called up to him. "Uh . . . how you get in?"

The wasp looked at Z as if he made a bad smell.

"Er, I'm afraid this is a private function," he said, embarrassed to have to explain it to this clueless, no-class little intruder.

In swooped his mate. "Who are your friends, dear?" she asked him.

"Crawling insects, poopsie," he replied dismissively.

"Ohhh. The poor dears." She buzzed down closer to Bala and Z. "Good morning!" she said very slowly, as if they were very stupid. Then she flew closer to her mate.

"Darling, really," he whimpered in an undertone that Bala and Z could hear. "Greeting every insect that emerges out of the grass—"

Bala stepped forward, smiling. She'd clear up this little misunderstanding in no time. "Pardon me," she said. "I guess you don't recognize me. I've been traveling and I'm all . . . schlumpy. I'm Princess Bala."

"Oh, it's even worse," the male murmured to his mate. "They're Eurotrash."

His mate looked at the ants pityingly. "Darling, they're poor, they're dirty, they're smelly—we have to help them." She buzzed down to the two ants again. "If you'll just wait right here, we'll fetch you a little something," she told them.

"Oh, please, Muffy," said the male, "not another crusade."

"Chippie," she replied, "we have a social obligation to the less fortunate. I know you laugh at my hobbies, but this is *important* to me!"

He smiled indulgently. "You have such a big heart," he cooed at her. "That's why you're my little cuddlywiddles!"

The wasps were now completely involved in one another, ignoring Z and Bala.

"My big strong pheromone factory!" Muffy purred.

"You're my Muffy lovekins," he buzzed.

"Oh, brother," said Z. "Suddenly I've lost my appetite." He turned away. "You know, I guess I had imagined Insectopia—I don't know—a little differently."

Meanwhile, Muffy had buzzed over to where the food was, to get a snack for her needy little friends. She was so intent on finding something good, she did not notice the giant swatter that was whooshing through the air toward her.

Wham!

Chip flew to the side of his fallen mate. "Oh! Muffy! No! Oh no!" he wailed.

But she didn't move. She was squished.

There was no time to mourn, though, because the huge thing was slicing through the air again. "Look out!" screamed Z.

Chip quickly darted out of range as the thing landed squarely on Bala and Z. *Wham!*

But they were saved! They were so small, they went right through the holes of the swatter.

They were about to breathe a sigh of relief when a thunderous *BOOM* shook the ground. It was gigantic, bigger than anything Z had ever seen before. It rose up and hovered in the air for a split second, about to stomp the fleeing Bala. Then it slammed into the ground.

Z didn't know it, but the enormous thing was a human foot. As it rose again, Z could see that Bala was stuck to the bottom. In between the deep black ridges that covered its bottom surface, there was a great big blobby mass of sticky pink stuff, and Bala was all mucked up in it.

"Z! Help me!" she shrieked.

He watched helplessly as she was carried off on the foot in a huge, looping motion.

BOOM. The foot fell again as it tried to step on Z. Fortunately, it missed him. He was frantic. How was he going to save her from the pink goop?

Bala was screaming. "Z! Get me out of heeere!"

The foot seemed to be moving away, and Z's heart sank. How would he keep up with it?

Just then, he realized that the other foot was rising as it walked away. He saw a dangling ropelike thing hanging from it. As it rose, Z made a determined run for it, and at the last moment caught on to the snaky, swinging rope.

The foot lifted off into the air, with Z hanging on for dear life. He could see the landscape rolling and pitching crazily beneath him as he went higher and higher and higher. It was carrying him farther and farther away from Bala.

"Bala!" he cried. "This is not good!"

For a moment, the foot seemed to pause in the air, and then it descended again, sending Z into a stomach-churning free fall. Meanwhile, the foot on which Bala was stuck rose up again.

Z, trying to keep his lunch down, was on the descent. *BOOM*. And then the terrifying ascent into the sky again. It was now or never.

With a mighty swing, he flung himself off the rope he was holding onto, sailed through the air, and caught the one on the monster's other foot. The momentum swung him up and under, so that he smashed into the pink stuff next to Bala. Now he was stuck too.

"Hi," he said to her, his voice shaky with fear.

Z and Bala had just enough time to hold hands and scream as the ground rose to meet them. *THUD!* They were squashed deeper into the wad of pink stuff.

A terrified Bala clutched Z as they began the dizzying rise again. "Z?" she said in a trembling voice.

"Yes?"

"It looks like this is it, just when I was starting to like you." She gripped his arm as the gigantic foot rose, and they got ready for the inescapable fall . . . but it didn't come. They just hovered there, high in the air.

Just then, a monstrous hand approached, holding a round, flat, copper-colored disk as big as a mountain. The huge image of a bony-cheeked man with a beard stared down at them.

"Who the heck is *that*?" screamed Z.

With the helpless ants trapped in it, the goo was transferred to the huge disk, which was then flung away. Flying through the air for what seemed like miles, they turned over and over in a lopsided orbit, screaming. Then they landed with a crash in total darkness.

CHAPTER

General Mandible stood in his chambers. In the center of the room sat Weaver, tied to a chair. His face looked dreadful. It had been punched many times. Cutter stood by, just watching the interrogation.

"That's enough," Mandible said to the soldier who was giving Weaver the once-over.

"I ain't telling you nothing!" said Weaver.

"Soldier," said Mandible, "the Princess is vital to the future of this colony. She must be returned to take her proper place as queen."

"We already have a queen," said Weaver.

"As for your friend Z," Mandible continued, ignoring Weaver, "why should I hurt him? He's not important. We all know that one individual ant doesn't matter. Not you . . . not Cutter . . . not even her."

He extended his hand to the doorway, so that Weaver could see Azteca being dragged in by a couple of soldiers.

"Azteca!" cried Weaver.

"Don't tell that jerk anything," Azteca said defiantly.

"Where is Z?" Mandible demanded of Weaver.

The soldier who had been punching Z cracked his knuckles, looking at Azteca.

"I don't know where he is!" cried Weaver in anguish. He didn't want to tell them anything, but he was afraid for Azteca. What would they do to her if he didn't talk?

"That's too bad," said Mandible. He waved again, and the soldier advanced on Azteca.

"Wait!" Weaver shouted. "Insectopia!"

Mandible and Cutter turned and stared at Weaver.

"Look, I know it sounds crazy. But that's where he'd be going."

Cutter stepped forward. "Soldier, you think this is a game?" he asked, glaring at Weaver. "Insectopia does not exist."

But before Cutter could go on, General Mandible's voice cut in. "As a matter of fact, it does," he said coolly.

"Sir?" said Cutter, astonished.

"I'll brief you on the coordinates," said the general. "You're going to bring the Princess back. As for Z, kill him."

"But—you said—he didn't matter!" cried Weaver.

"It's for the good of the colony," Mandible said with a little smile. "You made the right decision."

Weaver could do nothing but hang his head in shame. He had let this evil general outsmart him. He had betrayed his friend. Weaver was demolished.

"Gentlemen," said Mandible, full of energy, "now you see how dangerous individualism can be. It makes us . . . vulnerable." He turned to the guards. "Take him back to the Mega-Tunnel. Put him on the front line. Dismissed."

Mandible held out a pick to Weaver. Weaver, completely and publicly broken, took it without argument.

Z had finally pried himself loose from the pink goo. Now he just had to get Bala free.

"Geez, what was I thinking?" said Z. "I almost got you killed!" He tugged on her arm.

"You know, you really shouldn't be so hard on yourself."

Z set his jaw. "That's it. I'm taking you back to the colony." He gave her a good hard pull, and she came popping out, knocking them both over in the process.

"Insectopia," said Z. "I must've been crazy."

Bala, who had tumbled beyond him, lifted herself onto one elbow. She was staring at something a little distance away. "Z?" she said.

"But you know what?" he continued, pacing behind her. "I can admit when I'm wrong—"

"Z!"

Z kept pacing, into his speech. "And this time, I gotta tell you, I was—"

She couldn't stand it anymore. She grabbed him by the shoulders and spun him around, so he would see what she was seeing.

"—absolutely, one hundred percent . . . correct," he said, gazing at it in awe. "Have you ever seen anything more beautiful in your life?"

"Z . . . it's . . . it's . . . *Insectopia!*"

"Shhh!" he hushed her. "Don't jinx it!" He grabbed her hand. "C'mon," he said.

There it was, just as they had dreamed it would look. No. Better. All the stuff to eat an insect could want, just there for the taking. No armies, no wars, no Mega-Tunnel. Just garbage, garbage, garbage, as far as the eye could see.

They danced in it. They slid down it. They ate and

drank to their hearts' content. And there was nobody to tell them what to do. Nobody but the residents of Insectopia, all living together in peace and harmony.

The Mega-Tunnel was coming along nicely. Mandible was pleased. On the table in his chamber was a progress chart, showing that it was almost completed.

At this moment, he was briefing a group of his most trusted officers. "All right, everybody, I want all teams in place, fully prepared, ready to seal the doors. Here and here." He stabbed at the map. "Make certain the digging crew stays on schedule for the breakthrough midway in the dedication ceremony."

When the officers were gone, Mandible stood alone and continued to stare at the map. He stared hardest at the thing at the end of the tunnel. Just beyond it, according to the chart, was some sort of bowl-like depression in the earth. Something that could have been a body of water, perhaps. But only Mandible knew what it was.

Outside, Cutter was searching for the Princess. He was armed with state-of-the-ant weaponry and festooned with leaves and branches. On top of it all, he wore a determined expression. He was going to carry out his mission, no matter what.

87

Back in Insectopia the insects were having a cook-out. Unaware of their pursuer, Bala and Z were sitting together with their new companions, enjoying the warm glow of the fire. They were munching on something brown.

"This stuff tastes like garbage," said the ladybug.

"Well, it *is* garbage," said the fly.

"Hey, you guys, somebody needs to feed that fire," said the fly lazily.

"Dude," said the mosquito, "I did it last time."

"Well, I'm not gonna do it," the fly said. "It's not my job."

"What about the new guy? He hasn't contributed yet," said the ladybug, pointing to the ant couple sitting at the edge of the circle, deep in conversation.

". . . and he just died in my arms, like that," Z was telling Bala quietly. "You know, I don't think he ever once in his life made his own choice."

"I never knew it was like that," she mused. "I mean, up in the palace, well, I guess we just let the general make all the decisions."

"Let me ask you something," Z said. "What made you come to the bar that night?"

She thought about it. "I guess I was looking for a little trouble." She giggled.

"Well, trouble is my middle name." He smiled back. "Actually, my middle name is Marion, but I don't want you to spread that around."

"You're pretty strange. You do know that, don't you?"

"Well—strange is not exactly the word I would use."

"I like it," she said, snuggling a little closer. "You're not like anyone else."

"In that case—actually, now that you mention it . . . there is a certain strangeness to me, you know a kind of bizarre quality, some have said I'm freaky, but you know, I think it's complimentary . . ."

His words trailing off, Z leaned in to give Bala a kiss.

Just then, the fly yelled over to them, breaking in on their moment.

"Hey, new guy! We need more wood!"

"I'll be right back," Z said to Bala as he got up. "Just hold that thought—whatever it is you were thinking." He turned to the fly. "You ever wonder why they call you guys 'pests'?" he asked.

While he was gone, Bala sat in dreamy, contented silence and listened to the meandering conversation of the other insects.

"What if, like, we're just these tiny little things, and we're just, like, part of this whole other huge universe that's, like, so big we don't even know it exists?" said the mosquito.

The ladybug poked at the fire. "Man, that is so deep . . ."

While this philosophical discussion was going on, Z was looking for firewood. "Perfect," he griped to himself. "Nothing like a little manual labor on the most romantic night of my life."

Pretty soon he found a great piece of lumber, nice and straight. It looked okay, even though it had a sort of red bulb on the end of it. He began dragging it toward the clearing by its end, straining with the effort.

He glanced up at the sky, just as a shadow went gliding over him with a strange whooshing sound. He didn't give it much thought, though. There was all kinds of strange stuff out here.

But the fact was, the shadow belonged to a huge winged ant loaded down with weapons. It was Cutter. He landed smack in the middle of the clearing, and did some quick visual reconnaissance.

"Hi," he said to the mosquito, just as friendly as anything. "I was in the neighborhood and I thought I'd drop in." He scanned the clearing as he spoke, looking for Bala. "This is very . . . bohemian," he said.

Cutter kicked a little pile of junk out of the way.

"Aloha, dude," said the mosquito. "Welcome to Insec—"

Cutter shot out a fist and knocked him cold. He didn't even watch him fall.

"Sorry for interrupting," he said to the others. "Look, I'm hoping you people might help out me and the folks back home. You see . . . our princess has gone missing, and—well, we're just sick about it. She was about yea tall, fairly easy on the eyes. Anybody seen her?"

All the insects pointed at Bala, who was trying to sneak away unnoticed. "She's right there," they said in helpful unison.

Aha! Cutter lost no time in grabbing her. "Don't worry, Princess," he said. "You'll be back home soon!"

"Listen, Cutter, I'm—I'm not going back."

"The thing is, Princess," he told her, not loosening his grip, "I got orders."

"Orders? Well, *I'm* ordering you to head back alone."

"Wow. That was, well, very impressive," he said, looking suitably impressed. "Where's Z?"

"Oh, Z?" said the fly, ever helpful in true Insectopian fashion. "He's, uh—"

Bala cut him off sharply, before he could say anymore. "*Dead*," she finished for him. "Z's dead. You don't need to worry about him."

"Z's dead? Well, he was an ant with ideas," said Cutter dismissively. "Too bad for him. Let's go, Princess."

Cutter lifted off, dragging Bala up into the air with him.

"Cutter! Stop this!" she screamed.

Z, hauling his lumber back to the campfire, heard her scream. He looked up, just in time to see them overhead. "Bala!" he yelled, running after them. "Stop!" But it was too late. They were already flying off into the night sky.

Z stopped running. "Oh, no!" he wailed. "What am I going to do?" He took a deep breath and collected himself. "Okay—all right, let's be rational about this," he told himself. "Bala and I . . . well, she's a princess and I'm a soil relocation engineer."

Who was he fooling? Not himself, certainly. "On the other hand," he said to himself, "I gotta go back for her."

As he turned to go after her, he heard a strange booming voice from the edge of the clearing. "I'll give you a lift," said a voice.

Z looked around to see who had spoken, and spotted a bottle of something brown and sharp-smelling, lying on its side. And inside the bottle was Chip.

"It's the least I can do," said Chip, emerging from the bottle and sounding normal. "And besides"—his voice choked up—"it's what my waddlykiddles would want."

Chip was talking funny. He was walking funny, too. Z was glad to see him, and happy to have the offer of help, but frankly, the idea of flying Air Chip made him a little nervous. And there was also that fear of heights to think about.

"Look," said Z, "how about a cuppa joe first? You know, I think I saw a puddle of coffee over there."

Chip stood up a bit straighter and tried weaving less. "Well, old boy," he said, "saddle up!"

And off they flew—not in a straight line, but in the general direction of the colony.

CHAPTER

11

Mandible's chamber, high above the rest of the colony, was now a hive of activity. Underlings rushed back and forth, making last-minute preparations, while Mandible mapped out the plan with his junior officers. Things would be coming to a head soon.

Mandible looked up with a little smile when he saw Cutter enter, dragging Bala with him. "Ah, Princess! You're just in time."

He turned to dismiss his officers. "Outstanding. Wait for my signal," he said.

Bala struggled against Cutter's grip. "Take your hands off me," she commanded.

Of course, that didn't happen. "General, what exactly is going on here? I demand an explanation," she snapped.

"I'll explain everything," said the general. "Afterwards." He motioned to a nearby officer. "Is the southeast entrance secured?"

"Yes, sir."

"Not 'afterwards.' Now!" Bala yelled at her fiancé. She shoved some of the maps off the tabletop onto the floor. The room went silent.

"I don't like the way you think," she continued, "and I don't like the way you run this colony, and I don't like *you*. The wedding is off." He just looked at her. "Things are going to change around here," she added.

For a moment, the officers were frozen in place, wondering which way the duel of wills was going to go. Then Mandible smiled.

"You're right, Princess. Things *are* going to change." He caught Cutter's eye. "Why don't we make her more . . . comfortable?" he suggested. "Since she'll be in here for a while."

Cutter pushed Bala down into a chair.

"What do you think you're doing? My mother will have your head!" the Princess yelled.

"I doubt that," said the general.

He looked at her for a minute, regarding her with new interest. "You've got a fighter's spirit, Bala. And that's just what we need to start our new colony. We will rinse away all the filth from our gutters. We'll start anew, with you by my side as my queen."

"You're *crazy!*"

"I believe history will see things differently," he said, unruffled.

He turned once more to his officers. "All right, gentlemen. Time to take your positions."

He and the others marched out. "Someday you'll thank me," he told Bala just before he shut the door, locking her in his office.

Outside, as they approached their destination, Z clung desperately onto Chip's back.

"Chip, look out!" cried Z as they came within inches of the ground. They gained a little altitude, and then Z saw the colony. "There it is!" he said.

"Oh, oh yeah," mumbled Chip. He took another dive, crash-landing at the entrance.

"Well, then go get the woman you love, Z," said the wasp.

"So long, Chip. Thanks."

They shook hands, and Chip felt himself filling with emotion. For the first time he understood why Muffy enjoyed helping those in need. As a smile crept across his face, he nodded to Z and flew off. Z turned and headed for the entrance.

There were lots of guards at the entrance, but they seemed to be worried more about people getting out than in. Z decided to try sneaking past the group at the nearest entrance.

"You there! Where do you think you're going?"

"Me? I, uh—"

"You're not supposed to be out here! All workers are to report to the tunnel opening ceremonies!"

"Yes, of course, the tunnel opening ceremonies. Better get going." Z waltzed nonchalantly inside.

He proceeded through the main chamber, where more soldiers were massed. Something was sure going on, something really big. Something not good. But what was it?

"Hey!" barked a guard.

"I'm going . . . tunnel opening ceremonies," mumbled Z.

"Get moving."

And move he did, sidling through the mass of uptight soldiers, trying not to notice their hostile glances. "Going to the tunnel opening ceremonies," he kept saying.

"Hey, worker!" yelled a soldier farther inside.

"Opening the tunnel . . . they need me . . . I'm a key man," he mumbled inanely.

"Where do you think you're going?" demanded the soldier.

"tunnelopeningceremonies . . . opening the tunnel. Tunopcermies," he babbled frantically.

The soldier waved him on, disgusted. Workers.

Z made his way on, and soon he heard Bala's voice, very faintly. She was yelling her head off, it sounded like. He sneaked forward, and realized that he was in the area right below Mandible's office.

He made his way up, listening to the sound of Bala's voice growing louder. Turning a corner, he stopped just in time to avoid being seen by a burly guard who was posted in front of the general's door.

Z considered his options. There was only one, he realized. He began to make his way onto the narrow ledge outside the window.

Meanwhile, Bala was still yelling. "Hey, come on, lemme out of here! You're gonna be in big trouble, you hear me? Big trouble. Big, big, big trouble. Are you listening out there? I am the Princess!" She hurled a chair through the window.

Then Z's head poked through the window.

"Your manners haven't improved much," he teased her.

"Z! It's you! You came back for me!"

"Yeah, I came back for you. I have strong feelings for you. Let's face it—you're beautiful. A little combative at times, but I think we can work on that—"

Bala pulled him toward her. "You talk too much," she said, kissing him.

"I think I'm about to become the strong silent type," he said.

They heard the guard stirring outside the door. "C'mon," said Z. "The city's deserted, we better get out of here."

"Z, we can't go. Mandible's insane. He keeps talking about washing away the filth, and changing history, and—I think he's going to try to kill my mother!"

While she'd been talking, Z had been looking at one of the maps Bala had thrown to the floor. He looked grim. "Not just your mother," he said. "Everyone!"

"What's going on?" she said, really frightened now.

He showed it to her on the map. "Look . . . here we are safe in the city, but they're gonna seal everyone off in the Mega-Tunnel. Here's the lake . . ." His finger traced the tunnel's path, right into the lake. Suddenly, Z knew exactly what the general was planning. The general's chosen few would be spared, and everyone else would be drowned in the tunnel.

"You're right!" he said to her agitatedly. "We can't leave now. C'mon, we gotta get down there."

Bala reached out and took his hand.

In the Mega-Tunnel, the opening ceremonies had begun. Mandible, standing by the podium with the Queen, gestured to the crowd for silence.

"Today," he declared, "is the realization of a dream. A dream of a proud colony. A pure colony. A colony reborn."

Not knowing any better, the crowd began applauding.

"We have worked together," he continued, "and built a pathway to our future. When this tunnel opens, the past will be washed away . . . and a new day will dawn!"

As the crowd cheered wildly, Mandible nodded to his audience and then backed away from the podium.

The Queen was not applauding. "A stirring speech, General. I only wish my daughter were here to appreciate it."

"I know how concerned you are about Bala, Your Majesty," he said. "But my scouts are on her trail and it's only a matter of time before they catch up to her."

"General," she interrupted, "I don't want to discuss it. Just find her."

"I will, Your Highness." He saluted her and turned away. She was of no interest to him.

Meanwhile, Z and Bala were racing frantically through the colony. They were blocked at every turn by soldier ants guarding the doorways.

At the podium, Mandible ordered Cutter and the troops, "Seal up the door."

Cutter did not respond to Mandible. He was looking over the crowd.

"Cutter, did you hear me?" Mandible repeated.

"Sir," said Cutter, "I've been thinking. Do we need to go through with this? Look at what these workers have done. They've got the right stuff. Isn't there any other way?"

Mandible was frowning now. "Cutter, you're a fine officer. You have discipline. Courage. Ability. But you seem to have a certain weakness for the lower orders that I find disturbing. Now, are you with me?"

Cutter, hearing the general's tone, snapped right out of it. What had he been thinking? Sympathy for the workers was *not* a good career move.

"Yes, sir. I apologize," he said, back to his old self.

"All right, then. Seal it up," said the general.

The Queen was now in the middle of her own speech to the workers. "As I look out on this magnificent tunnel, I am filled with pride. In these difficult times, it is of great solace to know that you workers—"

"MOM! Wait!" It was Bala, yelling from the opposite side of the tunnel, across the crowd.

But the Queen was too far away to hear. She kept going with her speech, unaware of the disaster that awaited them all.

Z looked down the Mega-Tunnel and saw the lead team of workers in the distance, readying to break through at the front.

"Every worker in the colony is here!" he shouted to Bala, looking at the huge crowd. "Go warn your mother! I've got to get to those diggers before they break through."

"There's not enough time!" she cried.

"Hey, leave the pessimism to me, okay?" He kissed her and ran off.

Elbowing past the workers, who were all craning to look at the Queen, Z made his way toward the end of the tunnel. " 'Scuse me, pardon me," he kept saying, with very little effect.

"Watch it, you jerk!" said one of the workers, gesturing toward their monarch, who was still talking.

"This tremendous accomplishment," she was saying, "is a testimony to the strength of our tireless workers! It is not often enough—"

"Mom! Mom! Stop!" screamed Bala at the top of her lungs.

The Queen turned, finally, and saw her.

"Bala! Where have you been? Are you all right?"

"I'm okay."

"What happened?"

"Mother," said Bala frantically, "we're in terrible danger!" She hurriedly explained the situation to the Queen, trying to make it as simple as possible. She told her about Mandible's evil plan. "We're all going to drown!" she said urgently. "This tunnel is going to flood!"

"Then we've got to get everyone out of here!" the Queen cried.

CHAPTER

12

At that moment, at the top of the tunnel, the lead digging crew was making the final breakthrough to what they imagined was the surface. And at the very head of that crew, first in line for a watery death, was Weaver, placed there by the vindictive Mandible.

Weaver looked utterly defeated—tamed and dead-eyed, chipping away at the wall. Mandible had robbed him of his spirit. As he cast his eyes over the other workers, he hardly seemed to register that Azteca was standing nearby. She tried to catch his eye, but he just looked away.

"Put your backs into it, people!" yelled the foreman.

Weaver reared back with his huge pick, taking a mammoth swing toward the wall.

"WAIT!" cried a voice. "Stop digging!"

The voice was somehow familiar. Like a batter checking his swing, Weaver held up—but it was too little, too late. His pick landed with a thunk, embedded in the wall.

Weaver turned and saw a figure running toward him. "Z?!" he said.

Z moved forward, pushing aside the foreman.

"Is that you?" said Weaver in wonderment.

"Weaver, stop!" Z gasped. "Hold up, everyone! Stop—stop digging!"

"On whose authority?" demanded the foreman.

"On your own authority!" shouted Z. "If you break through that wall, we're all going to drown!"

"Look, I got orders, and those orders say dig," the foreman argued.

"What if someone ordered you to jump off a bridge, and . . . oh, brother, I'm asking the wrong guy here . . ."

The crew of digging ants glanced at each other nervously, then looked to the foreman for orders. Meanwhile, water droplets were cascading down from the ceiling like a small rain shower.

"Look!" said Z, pointing to the water. "Think for yourselves!"

"Give me that!" said the foreman, grabbing some-one's pick. "I've had enough outta you! Get back to work!" He heaved the pick and sank it into the wall, hard.

Weaver was standing still, listening to something. "What's that noise?" he said.

Then they all heard it: the menacing *hissss*. Water was starting to spray out from around the foreman's pick.

"Uh-oh," said the foreman.

"Run!" shouted Z.

But before anybody could go anywhere, the pick came exploding out of the wall. Weaver barely had time to yank Azteca out of the way.

"Let's get out of here!" yelled Weaver.

They all started stampeding away from the wall. Behind them, the water was starting to make a huge crack in the wall. The spray was becoming a geyser.

The strong voice of the Queen rang through the Mega-Tunnel. "Everyone, listen to me," she said into the microphone. "We've all been deceived. We need to calmly head toward the exits—"

Not likely. The ants filling the tunnel were already panicking, climbing over one another in the rush to get out.

"No! Don't panic! Don't—"

A horde of terrified ants rushed headlong past the Queen, nearly knocking her over. End of speech.

At the front of the tunnel, some of the ants from the work crew, fleeing the tidal wave of water, tripped and fell and were consumed by it.

"Every ant for himself!" screamed somebody.

And now, the ants who had been lucky enough to make it to the exits without being trampled were making a new discovery: all the exits were blocked! They were trapped!

The ants began to cluster together on a rise in the center of the chamber, surrounded by the flood that rushed toward them from all sides. Weaver, Z, and Azteca made it to the temporary safety of the central mound.

"What are we going to do?" cried Bala.

"There's nothing we *can* do!" said the foreman.

The crowd murmured in panic-stricken agreement. They were going to die here as the water rose to engulf them.

Z, panicked like everybody else, looked around him for some ray of hope, some way to get out of here. Then he looked—up.

"Yes, there is! There is something we can do!" he

yelled. "Weaver, give me a leg up!"

With Weaver's help, he climbed onto the big soldier's shoulders and shouted to the terrified crowd as the water continued to rise.

"Everyone! Listen to me!"

"Who the heck are you?" some worker ant in the crowd yelled.

"He's Z!" Bala yelled back.

This got the crowd's attention.

"Listen," said Z. "We gotta help each other get out of here before we all drown!"

"How?"

"By making a ladder!" Z answered.

The ants all looked at each other. They were nervous. They were dubious. They were scared.

"Hey, if we built this," said Z, gesturing at the Mega-Tunnel, "we can do anything!"

This had some effect. The ants begin to look positive. They moved forward, willing and wanting to participate. They just needed someone to show them how. After all, they were worker ants, accustomed to following orders.

But Z knew just what they had to do. "Okay, let's move it!" he said.

"I'm on it," said Weaver, grinning beside him. He began barking out orders. "All of you! Gather round me! You! Start climbin'!

The worker ants immediately snapped into perfectly coordinated action, doing what they were so good at—only this time, it was to save their own lives. "You grab hold!" said one ant to the next. "Move it! Move it!"

Bracing himself, the big soldier planted his legs firmly on the ground as other ants started filing forward, climbing onto Weaver's back, linking arms together so others could climb up. A ladder to the ceiling started building, on the backs and shoulders of the ants themselves.

The Queen was now standing in the water near the base of the ladder, holding back.

"Excuse me, Your Majesty," said Azteca, hoisting her up to where she was grabbed by some more workers and carried along.

Bala was right behind her. She looked at Z in anguish, torn. "Z, I've gotta help my mom," she said.

"Don't worry, I know almost exactly what I'm doing," said Z with a smile. "I'll see ya at the top."

Behind them, a wave of water crashed against the crowd. There were screams and groans.

Bala started climbing.

Outside, Mandible was inspecting what remained of his army. The troops were organized in neat, if sparse, ranks.

109

"Gentlemen, there comes a time in the evolution of a perfect colony, when the strong are meant to rise above the weak. Now is that time."

Cutter stood in his usual place next to Mandible. But as the general spoke, a look of growing concern spread across Cutter's face. The soldiers cast uneasy glances at one another.

"We are the strong!" Mandible continued. "The chosen! And this place, the very ground at our feet, will be embraced by history. Below us, right now, the weak elements of the colony are being washed away."

This was not far from the truth. As ants making up the ladder strained toward the roof of the tunnel, the whole structure teetered atop Weaver's sturdy legs. The ant on the very top could barely reach the ceiling. He began to dig.

Meanwhile, the water was still rising. By now it was lapping at the necks of Weaver, Azteca, and Z. And now the word was passed down the ladder to them: the ants were not quite high enough to break through the roof!

"Oh my God, we're not going to make it! We need more ants!" cried Z.

"You two," said Weaver to his friends. "Get up there!" He was shaking with the effort of holding up the whole ladder.

"Weaver, you can't hold it alone!" said Azteca.

"Get going," said Weaver through gritted teeth.

Z could see that there was no point in arguing, not now. Their only hope was to break through the ceiling, and fast. "Hang in there, buddy!" he said to Weaver. Azteca leaned over and gave Weaver a kiss. And with that, she and Z clambered all the way up the bridge, to the very top. There, Z stood on Azteca's shoulders, stretching up to reach the roof.

"Got it!" he said.

"Start digging!" said Azteca. "Hurry!"

Down below, the water was now at Weaver's nose. He began to hold his breath.

Z started scraping away at the roof, working furiously to break through.

Outside, Mandible was still giving his speech. This was his great moment. He was loving it. "Our princess is secured," he crowed, "and our glorious future is at hand. We can all stand proud! It's time for a new beginning!"

The soldiers, however, didn't look awfully proud. Cutter, in particular, looked troubled.

And then Mandible looked down at the ground, right below his feet. There, it seemed, a hole was opening up.

"What the heck is that?" he said.

Just then, a large section of the ground opened up. Mandible had to jump aside to avoid falling into it. The dirt cascaded into the hole, tumbling past the tower of ants and splashing into the waters below.

Cutter walked over to the hole. Looking down, he could see the enormous structure that the worker ants had built with their own bodies. His eyes widened with surprise and admiration.

"I think that's the 'weak element' down there, sir," he said dryly.

Z was now stretching as far as he could, the ants giving it their all to boost him to the edge of the hole. As the army watched in amazement, Z's hand reached out of the hole, scrabbled around, and grabbed hold of the rim.

"Give—give me a hand," Z entreated the ants above.

Mandible went over to the edge. He paused; then he calmly stepped on Z's hand.

And only then did he look into the hole to see who it was. "Z?! You?" he spluttered.

At the bottom of the ladder, Weaver was still holding his breath, standing firm as the water rose above his head. He could not hear what was going on at the top of the ladder.

There Mandible stood, staring down at Z. "Let go! Don't you understand, it's for the good of the colony!"

"What are you saying?" said Z. "We *are* the colony!"

With a grunt, Mandible tried to push Z back down into the water below. But Cutter had now seen all he needed to see. He stepped forward and shoved Mandible aside. As Mandible stumbled, Cutter extended a hand down to Z.

"Cutter, what are you doing?" shouted Mandible.

"Something I should have done a long time ago. This is for the good of the colony, sir."

Mandible was now right at the edge of madness. "You useless, ungrateful maggot!" he shrieked. "I am the colony!" He charged toward Cutter.

"Look out!" Z warned Cutter, pushing him out of Mandible's way.

It was too late for Mandible to check his momentum. He crashed into Z, and they both went spinning downward into the hole, into the flood below. On the way down, Mandible was thrown against a sharp ledge—a blow that proved fatal.

"Z!" gasped Bala as he tumbled down toward the roiling water.

Above, Cutter turned to the soldiers. He was in command now. "Let's move it. Get these ants up here." The soldiers threw down their weapons and rushed over to the hole to pull the workers to safety.

A mighty cheer rose up as, hand over hand, the workers made their way up. Azteca, then the grateful Queen, and Bala emerged into the sunshine. The other ants poured out of the hole. Finally, they hauled a waterlogged Weaver up and onto the ground.

Meanwhile, the winged Cutter had zoomed down to the bottom of the hole. He dived beneath the surface of the churning water, searching frantically—not for his commanding officer, but for Z.

There he was! He plucked the limp little worker out of the water and rocketed back up with him.

Gently he laid the unconscious Z on the ground.

"Oh no! Z!" cried Bala, rushing to his side.

The worried crowd pressed in on them. "Back up, everybody, back up!" yelled Cutter. "Give the ant some air!"

Bala bent over Z and began desperately giving him mouth-to-mouth resuscitation. And finally, spluttering and coughing, Z came to.

"Yowch," he said, managing a smile at Bala.

"You did it!" said Bala.

"*We* did it," he said.

"You were so spectacular, so brave, so daring . . ."

"Don't forget virile," he added.

Weaver was now with them. "We made it, Z! You the ant!" Weaver pounded his friend on the back.

The ants begin to chant, even the soldiers: "Z! Z! Z! Z! Z!" They hoisted him onto their shoulders.

Z, as usual, could not just shut up. "Fellas, fellas, please, this is very embarrassing—"

Bala was hoisted up beside him. She threw her arms around him and gave him a big kiss. That shut him up. For a minute.

"On the other hand," he continued, "I probably could get used to this."

Z and Bala were passed from shoulder to shoulder as the ants cheered. In the crowd, Azteca and Weaver hugged happily. Z even got a big kiss on the cheek from the Queen herself.

EPILOGUE

And that was that.

It all certainly made a good story, some time later, when Z sat in the shade of a dandelion with his old friend Chip. They'd run into each other when Z was taking a little walk in the direction of the Monolith, just for old time's sake. And there he'd found Chip, buzzing about with his new girlfriend, Letitia.

"And there you have it," Z told Chip as he finished up the tale. "Your average boy-meets-girl, boy-likes-girl, boy-changes-underlying-social-order story." He paused a moment. "So, we rebuilt the colony. It's even better than before, because now it has a very large swimming pool.

Bala and I, incidentally, are thinking of starting a family. You know, just a few kids, a million or two to begin with."

Chip nodded sagely.

"I've got a great new therapist," Z continued. "He's been helping me get in touch with my inner maggot. I finally feel like I found my place, and, you know what? The funny thing is, it's right back where I started. The difference is, this time I chose it."

And way up in the tall buildings that circled their world, the people looked down into Central Park, unaware that they were looking down toward the ant who had single-handedly started a revolution and saved his whole colony.